THAT'S WHEN I'M
HAPPY!

Beth Shoshan
Jacqueline East

PaRragon

Bath · New York · Singapore · Hong Kong · Cologne · Delhi · Melbourne

There are some days
when I'm very happy...
and there are some days
when I'm a little bit sad.

But now, on those days
when I'm a little bit sad...
I try and find my way back
to being happy.

When it's cold outside

and my Daddy and I are clearing up…

And when we take a soft striped bag

and fill it up with leaves…

And when he chooses

one special leaf for me

because it's deeper, darker,

redder than all the others…

And when my Daddy

and I play soccer

through the leaves

and we're kicking

to each other

through a tunnel of trees...

...that's when I'm happy!

When it's cozy inside and my

Mommy and I give each other

great big bear hugs...

And when we rub our noses together...

And when she chooses one

special tickle, just for me

because it's wiggly,

squirmy, and makes me laugh

more than all the others...

And then my Mommy

gives me the biggest kiss of all...

And I reach up to give her a big kiss back...

 But not as big,

because my mouth is still very small...

...that's when I'm happy!

When it's night outside

and my Daddy and I gaze through the window...

And when he takes my hand

and points at the night sky...

And when he chooses one special star

for me because it's bigger,

burning brighter than all the others...

And then my Daddy
and I count all the stars
in the sky, and he says
there are more than 119…

But I can't count any higher…

…that's when I'm happy!

When it's warm inside and my Mommy

and I run our fingers through the books...

And when we look at all the pictures...

And when she chooses

one special book for me

because it's our favorite,

better than all the others...

And then my Mommy reads
the perfect story to me
and I can read some
of the words...

But mostly the ones
with the letters
from my name in them...

...that's when I'm happy!

When it's dark everywhere

and I cuddle up

to my Mommy and Daddy

(even though they're asleep)

still telling stories to myself,

watching stars in the sky,

bathed in all their kisses,

and dreaming of the deep

red leaves...

That's when we're happy!

For Joshua, Asher, and Hannah

B.S.

Thanks Vicki

J.E.

Text © Beth Shoshan 2005
Illustrations © Jacqueline East 2005

This edition published by Parragon in 2007
Parragon
Queen Street House
4 Queen Street
Bath BA1 1HE, UK

Published by arrangement with Meadowside Children's Books
185 Fleet Street, London, EC4A 2HS

ISBN 978-1-4054-9538-7
Printed in China